For Mom and Dad and Simon

With thanks to Paddington Pooka
for her example and assistance

Copyright © 1988 by Penny Dale

Second U.S. edition 1992
First published in Great Britain in 1988 by Walker Books Ltd., London.
ISBN 1-56402-104-1
Library of Congress Catalog Card Number 91-58763
Library of Congress Cataloging-in-Publication information is available

10 9 8 7 6 5 4 3 2 1

Printed in Hong Kong

Candlewick Press
2067 Massachusetts Avenue
Cambridge, Massachusetts 02140

Wake Up, Mr. B.!

Penny Dale

CANDLEWICK PRESS
CAMBRIDGE, MASSACHUSETTS

Rosie woke up very early.

She went to wake up Billy.

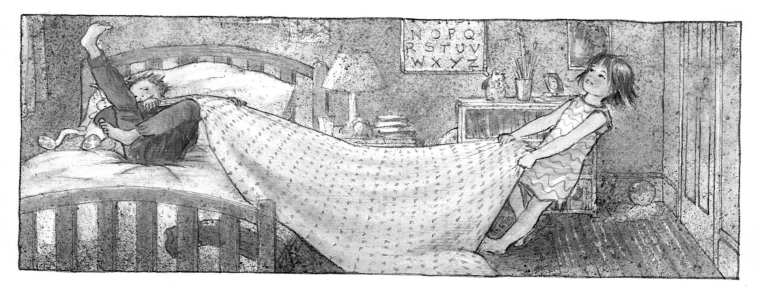

She went to wake up Dad.

She went to find Mr. B.

"Wake up, Mr. B.," she said.

"Come with me, Mr. B.," she said.

"Let's get dressed."

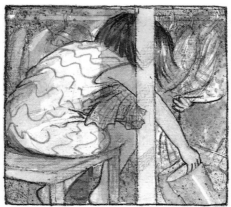

"Get in my car, Mr. B.," she said.

"We're driving to the sea."

"Get in my boat, Mr. B.," she said.

"We're sailing around the world."

"Get in my balloon, Mr. B.," she said.

"Don't fall asleep. We're flying to the moon."

"Come and see Rosie and Mr. B.," said Billy.

"Wake up, Rosie! Wake up, Mr. B.!"

2/93